First edition for the United States and Canada published 1999
by Barron's Educational Series, Inc.

Text and Illustrations copyright © Nicola Smee 1998

First published in Great Britain by Orchard Books in 1998.

All inquiries should be addressed to:
Barron's Educational Series, Inc.
250 Wireless Boulevard
Hauppauge, New York 11788
http://www.barronseduc.com

Library of Congress Catalog Card No.: 98-72771
International Standard Book No. 0-7641-0864-6

Printed in Italy

987654321

Freddie Learns
to Swim

Nicola Smee

• little • barron's •

I'd like to be able to swim like my fish.
So would Bear.

Mom takes us to the
swimming pool.

Not the big pool, the little learner's pool.

I'm ready!